Jame
AND THE BALLOONS

by Christopher Awdry

illustrated by Ken Stott

Heinemann · London

William Heinemann Ltd
Michelin House
81 Fulham Road
London SW3 6RB
LONDON · MELBOURNE · AUCKLAND
First published in 1990
First paperback edition 1991
Reprinted 1992
Copyright © William Heinemann Ltd 1990
ISBN 0 434 92629 9
Printed in Great Britain by
Cambus Litho, East Kilbride

There was to be a balloon race on the Island of Sodor.
All the engines were very excited.

"I love balloons," said Thomas, "especially at parties when they go pop."
Gordon chuckled.

"But these are not party balloons," said Gordon.
"They are hot-air balloons with baskets fixed to them.
They carry people up into the sky."

James was chosen to take the balloons to their starting point. He was very proud.

"I wish I could watch the balloon race," he said.
"So do I," said his driver. "But we can't stop. We have work to do."

Later that afternoon, as James puffed down the line, he saw the balloons gently rising into the air.

"Can't we stop and watch for a while?" James sighed.
"I'm sorry, James," said his driver. "We're already late, we
   must move on."

The balloons were high in the sky now. They drifted overhead, but one sank very low.

"It looks as if that balloon is in trouble," said James.
His driver slowed down.

The balloon was almost down now. It bumped along the ground and landed on the line right in front of James. His driver put the brakes on.

"Thank you for stopping in time," shouted one of the balloonists. "It looks as if we are out of the race though."

"Never mind," replied James's driver. "We'll take you and your balloon to the finish."

James's driver and fireman helped the balloonists to pack their gear away.

Then they all heaved the heavy bundle onto the train.

The balloonists climbed into the guard's van and James started off again.

James reached the finish just in time to see the other balloons landing.

Lots of children were there to cheer the winner.

Thomas and the Fat Controller were there too.

"This is much more exciting than party balloons,"
said Thomas. The Fat Controller agreed.

"And even more exciting if you rescue a balloon and bring it home," said James.

The Fat Controller laughed. "Well done, James," he said.